Call down the Moon

Other Books by Myra Cohn Livingston

ANTHOLOGIES

A Time to Talk: Poems of Friendship

Dilly Dilly Piccalilli: Poems for the Very Young

If the Owl Calls Again: A Collection of Owl Poems

I Like You, If You Like Me: Poems of Friendship

Lots of Limericks

Poems of Christmas

Riddle-Me Rhymes

Roll Along: Poems on Wheels

Why Am I Grown So Cold? Poems of the Unknowable

(MARGARET K. McELDERRY BOOKS)

ORIGINAL POETRY

Flights of Fancy and Other Poems

Higgledy-Piggledy: Verses and Pictures

I Never Told and Other Poems

Monkey Puzzle and Other Poems

Remembering and Other Poems

There Was a Place and Other Poems

Worlds I Know and Other Poems

(MARGARET K. McELDERRY BOOKS)

Call down the Moon

poems
of
music

selected by
MYRA COHN LIVINGSTON

MARGARET K. McELDERRY BOOKS

Margaret K. McElderry Books
An imprint of Simon & Schuster Children's Publishing Division
1230 Avenue of the Americas
New York, New York 10020

Copyright © 1995 by Myra Cohn Livingston

Book design by Ann Bobco
The text of this book is set in Elegant Garamond.

Printed in the United States of America

First edition

10 9 8 7 6 5 4 3 2 1

Library of Congress Cataloging-in-Publication Data

Call down the moon: poems of music / selected by Myra Cohn Livingston.— 1st ed.
      p. cm.
   Includes index.
   ISBN 0-689-80416-4
   1. Music—Poetry. I. Livingston, Myra Cohn.
PN6110.M7C35 1995
821.008'0357—dc20

                                                        95-8283
                                                        CIP
                                                        AC

TO MUSIC, TO BECALM A SWEET-SICK-YOUTH

Charms, that call down the moon from out her sphere,
On this sick youth work your enchantments here:
Bind up his senses with your numbers, so,
As to entrance his pain, or cure his woe.
Fall gently, gently, and a while him keep
Lost in the civil Wilderness of sleep:
That done, then let him, dispossessed of pain,
Like to a slumbering Bride, awake again.

Robert Herrick

Contents

I. The Singers

GERTRUDE

When I hear Marian Anderson sing,
I am a STUFFless kind of thing.

Heart is like the flying air.
I cannot find it anywhere.

Fingers tingle. I am cold
And warm and young and very old.

But, most, I am a STUFFless thing
When I hear Marian Anderson sing.

Gwendolyn Brooks

LULLABY

My mother's hand
Moves up and down my cheek
Leaving music in its place
And I shall hear it
When I sleep
Singing up and down my face.

Julia Cunningham

MAMA'S SONG

Mama hums a sea-song with her eyes;
a deep blue rising sea-song,
moving as her eyes move,
weaving foam across my face.

White gulls whirl overhead;
the sun washes back and forth,
and I am rocking . . .
rocking . . .
      like a boat
in the waves
      of her song.

Deborah Chandra

RAY CHARLES

do you
dig ray
charles

when the
blues are
silent

in his throat

& he rolls
up his
sleeves

Sam Cornish

MY VOICE

Sing, sing, voice of mine,
While there is something
You have not yet said.
You have said nothing at all.

Juan Ramón Jiménez
Translated by H. R. Hays

THE HEAVENLY SONG

I wonder if you were able then to sing?
When I rose up there
To the great heavens up there,
I had become frightfully exhausted,
I had become frightfully breathless.
But when I caught sight of my relations,
Is it you, who once were?
Then I took to singing high-soundingly,
That time I had been quite exhausted,
I breathed my little song about it.

Ammassalik Eskimo

ON A BAD SINGER

Swans sing before they die—'twere no bad thing
Should certain persons die before they sing.

Samuel Taylor Coleridge

MY SINGING AUNT

The voice of magic melody
    With which my aunt delights me,
It drove my uncle to the grave
    And now his ghost affrights me.
This was the song she used to sing
    When I could scarcely prattle,
And as her top notes rose and fell
    They made the sideboard rattle:

"What makes a lady's cheeks so red,
    Her hair both long and wavy?
'Tis eating up her crusts of bread,
    Likewise her greens and gravy.
What makes the sailor tough and gay?
    What makes the ploughboy whistle?
'Tis eating salt-beef twice a day,
    And never mind the gristle."

Thus sang my aunt in days gone by
    To soothe, caress, and calm me;
But what delighted me so much
    Drove her poor husband barmy.
So now when past the church I stray,
    'Tis not the night-wind moaning,
That chills my blood and stops my breath,
    But poor old uncle's groaning.

James Reeves

An opera star named Maria
Always tried to sing higher and higher,
    Till she hit a high note
    Which got stuck in her throat—
Then she entered the Heavenly Choir.

Anonymous

There was an old person of Tring
Who, when somebody asked her to sing,
    Replied, "Isn't it odd?
    I can never tell 'God
Save the Weasel' from 'Pop Goes the King'!"

Unknown

AUTUMN SONG ON PERRY STREET

Our soprano is on the wind tonight
our slightly off-coloratura.
She and the smell of vanilla
from the National Biscuit Co.
tell us the weather'll be chiller
and the leaves are due to blow.
Somehow the aria's never quite right,
though the areaways endure her
hour upon hour for weeks,
as the back-yard pump starts up
never to, ever to stop.
"One fine—"   "One fine day—" she shrieks
"One fine day he will come—" (Bravura.)
If her voice didn't carry, he might.

Lloyd Frankenberg

WON'T YOU COME HOME BILL BAILEY?

You liked vegetarian food
plus those old-time songs
that drove me up a wall

> THE RAIN IN SPAIN
> FALLS MAINLY ON THE PLAIN

I liked red meat (rare)
and rock music (hard)
I adored horror films
you loved books
and finally we split up
in four weeks

I gave back your books
you gave back my tapes
and that seemed to end it
except for one thing

> I AIN'T HAD NO LOVIN' SINCE
> JANUARY FEBRUARY JUNE AND JULY

those old-fashioned songs of yours
jumbling around in my head
like sneakers in a dryer
keeping me up day and night

REMEMBER THAT RAINY EVENING
I THREW YOU OUT
WITH NOTHING BUT A
FINE-TOOTH COMB?

Please come over right away
you gotta clean out this stuff

PLEASE RELEASE ME LET ME GO
I DON'T LOVE YOU ANYMORE

I mean it: I'm going nuts

Ralph Fletcher

I HEAR AMERICA SINGING

I hear America singing, the varied carols I hear,
Those of mechanics, each one singing his as it should be
   blithe and strong,
The carpenter singing his as he measures his plank or
   beam,
The mason singing his as he makes ready for work, or
   leaves off work,
The boatman singing what belongs to him in his boat,
   the deck-hand singing on the steamboat deck,
The shoemaker singing as he sits on his bench, the hatter
   singing as he stands,
The wood-cutter's song, the ploughboy's on his way in
   the morning, or at noon intermission or at sundown,
The delicious singing of the mother, or of the young wife
   at work, or of the girl sewing or washing,
Each singing what belongs to him or her and to none else,
The day what belongs to the day—at night the party of
   young fellows, robust, friendly,
Singing with open mouths their strong melodious songs.

Walt Whitman

THE MINSTREL BOY

The Minstrel Boy to the war is gone,
    In the ranks of death you'll find him;
His father's sword he hath girded on,
    And his wild harp slung behind him.

"Land of song!" said the warrior-bard,
    "Though all the world betrays thee,
One sword, at least, thy rights shall guard,
    One faithful harp shall praise thee!"

The minstrel fell! but the foeman's chain
    Could not bring his proud soul under;
The harp he loved ne'er spoke again,
    For he tore its chords asunder;

And said: "No chain shall sully thee,
    Thou soul of love and bravery!
Thy songs were made for the brave and free,
    They shall never sound in slavery!"

Thomas Moore

II. Keyboards and Strings

THE PIANO

There is a lady who plays a piano;
   She lets me listen if I keep still.
I love to watch her twinkling fingers
   Fly up and down in scale or trill.

I love to hear the great chords crashing
   And making the huge black monster roar;
I love to hear the little chords falling
   Like sleepy waves on a summer shore.

Here comes an army with drums and trumpets,
   Now it's a battlefield, now it's a fire;
Now it's a waterfall boiling and bubbling,
   Now it's a bird singing higher and higher.

Now in the moonlight watch the trees bending,
   Water-nymphs rise from the bed of a stream;
Now in the garden the fountains are playing
   And in the sunshine flowers sway and dream.

Sometimes Harlequin comes with sweet Columbine,
   Sometimes I see deserts and twinkling stars,
The goose-girl, the fairies, a giant, a pygmy,
   And dark muffled strangers in foreign bazaars . . .

All these I see when I hear that piano
   All these and many things more do I see,
While over the keyboard the lady's hands travel,
   Yet nothing she sings, and no word says she.

James Reeves

CONCERT

When Aunt Wessie played she
reached into the keys with heavy
arms as though rooting tomato
slips, sinking hands in to

the wrists and raking the dirt
smooth, humming as she worked.
Would awaken suddenly from her reverie
and plunge onto the keyboard jamming the

pedal in like an accelerator
and slapping chords over
the melody till
the whole room filled

and beat like a sounding board
and every note on the trellis of wires blurred.
Almost blind, she stayed alone
in her house on the mountain

while we worked off in the fields.
As her hearing failed
the TV blasted soap tragedy
all over the valley.

Robert Morgan

A farmer in Knox, Ind.,
Had a daughter he called Mar.
　　But the neighbors said "O,
　　We really must go,"
Whenever she played the p.

Anonymous

THE PIANO

I sit on the edge
of the dining room, almost
in the living room where my parents,
my grandmother, & the visitors
sit knee to knee along the chesterfield & in
the easy chairs. The room is full, & my feet
do not touch the floor, barely
reach the rail across the front
of my seat. "Of course
you will want Bobby to play."—words
that jump out from the clatter
of teacups and illnesses. The piano
is huge, unforgettable.
It takes up the whole end wall
of the living room, faces me down
a short corridor of plump
knees, balanced saucers, hitched
trousers. "Well when is
Bob going to play?"
one of them asks. My dad says,
"Come on, boy, they'd like you
to play for them," & clears
a plate of cake
from the piano bench. I walk between
the knees & sit down
where the cake was, switch on
the fluorescent light
above the music. Right at the first notes
the conversation returns to long tales

of weddings, relatives bombed out again
in England, someone's mongoloid
baby. & there I am at the piano
with no one listening or even
going to listen
unless I hit sour notes, or stumble
to a false ending.
I finish.
Instantly they are back to me. "What a nice
touch he has," someone interrupts
herself to say.
"It's the hands," says another.
"It's always the hands, you can tell
by the hands." & so I get up
& hide my fists
in my hands.

Frank Davey

Over Mom's piano keys
Franklin drizzles antifreeze.
Hasn't Mom the hottest keyboard
On the entire eastern seaboard?

X. J. Kennedy

There was a Young Lady whose chin
Resembled the point of a pin;
    So she had it made sharp,
    And purchased a harp,
And played several tunes with her chin.

Edward Lear

COMPENSATION

Simylos the harper played a night-long recital,
And of all the neighborhood only old Origen lived,
For he was deaf:
         and the gods, in their merciful wisdom,
Had granted him length of days in place of hearing.

Leonidas the Alexandrian
Translated by Dudley Fitts

LITTLE DAVID

Little David play on your harp,
Hallelu, hallelu,
Little David play on your harp,
Hallelu.

David was a shepherd boy,
He killed Goliath,
An' he shouted for joy.

Now, Joshua was the son of Nun,
He never stop,
'Till his work was done.

Little David play on your harp,
Hallelu, hallelu,
Little David play on your harp,
Hallelu.

Traditional Spiritual

III. Fiddles and Cellos

JACKY'S FIDDLE

Jacky, come give me thy fiddle,
If ever thou mean to thrive.
Nay, I'll not give my fiddle
To any man alive.

If I should give my fiddle,
They'll think that I'm gone mad,
For many a joyful day
My fiddle and I have had.

Unknown

DOG AND PAPA'S FIDDLE

Papa polishes his fiddle
With a flannel cloth,
Whistles up Dog, who
Settles in, loose and soft.

Papa tucks his fiddle
Under his whiskery chin.
Dog stretches and yawns;
The night songs begin.

Dog scratches his ear.
The old moon climbs.
Papa's boots tap—
Each marking time.

Fiddle yowls like an alley cat.
Dog opens one eye,
Then Papa gentles into
Music of melting sky.

Kristine O'Connell George

"Now just who," muses Uncle Bill Biddle,
"Drilled a dreadful big hole through my fiddle?
    When I play a folk air
    Air is all there is there
And my tune comes out minus its middle."

X. J. Kennedy

THE FAST FIDDLER

There was a fast fiddler from Middletown
Who fiddled hi-diddle-dee-diddle-down.
      As his foot kept on tapping
      His strings kept on snapping
Ping-ping-ping, till he put his old fiddle down.

John Ciardi

A FIDDLER

Once was a fiddler. Play could he
Sweet as a bird in an almond tree;
Fingers and strings—they seemed to be
Matched, in a secret conspiracy.
Up slid his bow, paused lingeringly;
Music's self was its witchery.

In his stooping face it was plain to see
How close to dream is a soul set free—
A half-found world;
And company.

His fiddle is broken.
Mute is he.
But a bird sings on in the almond tree.

Walter de la Mare

MUSEUM VIOLIN

Once in a month
your labelled case
is unlocked
and you are warmed
to a tuning
and a stretch of song
that keeps your wood and glue
tempered and you alive
if only barely.
But now, not comforted
I stand before your silence
listening
with Brahms, Vieuxtemps
Bach, Mozart, Bruch
and we are less
to have you mute.
Do you perhaps
on evenings when the larger tomb
is closed
release your voice?
Give me a sign!
The bow quivers as I wait.

Julia Cunningham

SONG FROM A COUNTRY FAIR

When tunes jigged nimbler than the blood
And quick and high the bows would prance
And every fiddle string would burst
To catch what's lost beyond the string,
While half afraid their children stood,
I saw the old come out to dance.
The heart is not so light at first,
But heavy like a bough in spring.

Léonie Adams

DON'T LET THAT HORSE

Don't let that horse
                         eat that violin
     cried Chagall's mother
                               But he
               kept right on
                       painting
And became famous
And kept on painting
                   The Horse With Violin In Mouth
And when he finally finished it
he jumped up upon the horse
                     and rode away
       waving the violin

And then with a low bow gave it
to the first naked nude he ran across

And there were no strings
                attached

Lawrence Ferlinghetti

CELLO

Leaning back,
pretending
to doze,
the cello
sighs secrets
of a wind-filled
forest held
deep in its
resonant
old hollow.

Madeleine Comora

A violincellist named Lee
Stood high as a sycamore tree
But try as he might
Because of his height
He bowed through the bend in his knee.

Carole Schoneman

FIDDLER JONES

The earth keeps some vibration going
There in your heart, and that is you.
And if the people find you can fiddle,
Why, fiddle you must, for all your life.
What do you see, a harvest of clover?
Or a meadow to walk through to the river?
The wind's in the corn; you rub your hands
For beeves hereafter ready for market;
Or else you hear the rustle of skirts
Like the girls when dancing at Little Grove.
To Cooney Potter a pillar of dust
Or whirling leaves meant ruinous drouth;
They looked to me like Red-Head Sammy
Stepping it off, to "Toor-a-Loor."
How could I till my forty acres
Not to speak of getting more,
With a medley of horns, bassoons and piccolos
Stirred in my brain by crows and robins
And the creak of a wind-mill—only these?
And I never started to plow in my life
That some one did not stop in the road
And take me away to a dance or picnic.
I ended up with forty acres;
I ended up with a broken fiddle—
And a broken laugh, and a thousand memories,
And not a single regret.

Edgar Lee Masters

AUTUMN SONG

Autumn's long sobbing
Violin throbbing
    A tuneless strain
Tears apart
My listless heart
    In monotonous pain.

Gasping for breath,
Pale as death,
    I long to sleep.
Each hour that chimes
Recalls my old times,
    And I weep.

And I give in
To the ill wind
    Of grief,
Blown here and there
As if I were
    A dead leaf.

Paul Verlaine
Translated by Lloyd Alexander

IV. Banjos and Guitars

THE GUITAR
La guitarra

The cry of the guitar
begins.
The crystals of dawn are
breaking.
The cry of the guitar
begins.
It's useless to stop it.
It's impossible to
stop it.
Its cry monotonous
as the weeping of water,
as the weeping of wind
over the snowfall.
It's impossible to
stop it.
It cries for
distant things.
Sand of the scalding South
seeking white camellias.
It mourns the arrow without target,
evening without morning,
and the first bird dead
upon the branch.
Oh, guitar!
Heart wounded
by five swords.

Federico García Lorca
Translated by Rachel Benson and Robert O'Brien

Esta guitarra que toco
Tiene boca y sabe hablar;
Pero le faltan los ojos
Para ayudarme a llorar.

This guitar that I play
Has a mouth and can talk
But its eyes are missing
To help me cry.

Unknown
Translated by Joseph F. Domínguez

Si me pongo yo a cantar　　If I begin to sing
Un año y sus doce meses,　For a whole year long
No me han de sentir enchar　Not once will I be heard
La misma canción dos veces.　Repeating the same song.

Unknown
Translated by Joseph F. Domínguez

THE SIX STRINGS

The guitar
makes dreams cry.
The crying of lost
souls
escapes from its round
mouth.
And like the tarantula
it weaves a huge star
to catch sighs
that float on its black
wooden tank.

Federico García Lorca
Translated by Donald Hall

Cada vez que tengo penas	Each time I feel sorrow
Se las cuento a mi guitarra,	I tell my guitar
Que son las penas más chicas	For sorrows are lighter
Cuando se dicen cantadas.	When told in a song.

Unknown

Translated by Joseph F. Domínguez

El tambor es tu retrato;
Que mete mucho ruido
Y si se mira por dentro,
Se encuentra que está vacío.

Your life is like a drum.
It makes a great noise,
But if you look inside
You find it hollow.

Unknown

Translated by Joseph F. Domínguez

TAVERN GUITAR PLAYING A *JOTA* TODAY

Guitarra del mesón que hoy suenas jota . . .

Tavern guitar playing a *jota* today,
a *petenera* tomorrow,
according to whoever comes and strums
your dusty strings,

guitar of the roadside inn,
you never were nor will you be a poet.

You're a soul uttering its lonely
harmony to passing souls . . .

And whenever a traveler hears you
he dreams of hearing a tune of his native town.

Joaquim Maria Machado
Translated by Charles Guenther

THE TAPE

Poor song,
    going around in your cassette
    over and over again, repeating
    the same old tune,
    can you breathe in there?

Come, song,
    going around in your cassette
    over and over again, break out!
    Let me play you
    fresh on my guitar!

Myra Cohn Livingston

THE BANJO PLAYER

There is music in me,
      the music of a peasant people.
I wander through the levee, picking my banjo
      and singing my songs of the cabin and the field.
      At the Last Chance Saloon I am as welcome as the
      violets in March;
      there is always food and drink for me there,
      and the dimes of those who love honest music.
      Behind the railroad tracks the little children
      clap their hands and love me as they love
      Kris Kringle.
But I fear that I am a failure.
      Last night a woman called me a troubadour.
      What is a troubadour?

Fenton Johnson

SLAVE QUARTER

I can hear banjos
Soft and light
Down in the courtyard
In the moonlight.

What are they playing?
I cannot know,
For players and music
Died long ago.

Carl Carmer

BANJO TUNE

Plunk-a-Plunk! Plunk-a-Plunk!
I sit in the attic on an old trunk.
        Plunk-a-Plunk!
Locked in the old trunk is my wife,
And she may be there for the rest of her life.
        Plunk-a-Plunk!
She screams, "Let me out of here, you fool!"
I say, "I will when your soup gets cool."
        Plunk-a-Plunk!
She screams, "Let me out or I'll bean you, brother!"
I say, "Now, come on, tell me another!"
        Plunk-a-Plunk!
To keep one's wife in a trunk is wrong,
But I keep mine there for the sake of my song.
        Plunk-a-Plunk!
My song is hokum, my song is bunk,
And there's just a wad of old clothes in this trunk;
Not even the junkman would want this junk!
        Plunk-a-Plunk!
        Plunk-a-Plunk!
          Plunk!

William Jay Smith

V.   The Woodwinds

INSCRIPTION FOR A STATUE OF PAN

Be still O green cliffs of the Dryads
Still O springs bubbling from the rock
                                    and be still
Manyvoiced cry of the ewes:
                        It is Pan
Pan with his tender pipe:
                        the clever lips run
Over the withied reeds
                        while all about him
Rise up from the ground to dance with joyous tread
The Nymphs of the Water
                        Nymphs of the Oaken Forest

Plato
Translated by Dudley Fitts

A PIPER

A piper in the streets to-day
Set up, and tuned, and started to play.
And away, away, away on the tide
Of his music we started; on every side
Doors and windows were opened wide,
And men left down their work and came,
And women with petticoats coloured like flame.
And little bare feet that were blue with cold,
Went dancing back to the age of gold,
And all the world went gay, went gay,
For half an hour in the street to-day.

Seumas O'Sullivan

LISTENING TO A WANDERER'S "WATER MELODY"

A lone boat, a sliver of moon facing the maple woods—
A wanderer's heart is entrusted to his flute.
Mountain views merge with thousand sheets of rain,
And the last chord fades as our tears fall.

Wang Ch'ang-ling
Translated by Joseph J. Lee

MELLOWNESS & FLIGHT
For Charlie Parker

ever heard Bird
flap his wings

ever heard him
play Lover Man
Laura
Just Friends

ever taken
his mellowness in
& felt

like
you were
flying
with him

shining like him

a bright blackbird
slicing blue sky

sweetly & freely

ever heard Bird
flap his wings

George Barlow

THE FLUTE

This childhood recollection moves me even now:
The day our village flutist, laughing, showed me how
To hold the flute to my unpractised mouth. And he,
Then, close against his heart, set me upon his knee;
Declared I was a master, rivaling his skill,
And shaped my childish lips, though all uncertain still.
He taught me how to breathe a long, pure note; and then,
With my young fingers in his knowing hands, again
And yet again he guided them until they could,
Of their own will, draw music from a tube of wood.

André Chénier
Translated by Lloyd Alexander

There was a Young Lady of Bute,
Who played on a silver-gilt flute;
    She played several jigs,
    To her uncle's white pigs,
That amusing Young Lady of Bute.

Edward Lear

A Tutor who tooted the flute
Tried to teach two young tooters to toot;
    Said the two to the Tutor,
    "Is it harder to toot, or
To tutor two tooters to toot?"

Carolyn Wells

From SONG FOR ST. CECILIA'S DAY

The soft complaining flute
    In dying notes discovers
The woes of hopeless lovers,
Whose dirge is whisper'd by the warbling lute.

John Dryden

From SONGS OF INNOCENCE

Piping down the valleys wild
Piping songs of pleasant glee
On a cloud I saw a child.
And he laughing said to me.

Pipe a song about a Lamb;
So I piped with merry chear,
Piper pipe that song again—
So I piped, he wept to hear.

Drop thy pipe thy happy pipe
Sing thy songs of happy chear,
So I sung the same again
While he wept with joy to hear

Piper sit thee down and write
In a book that all may read—
So he vanish'd from my sight.
And I pluck'd a hollow reed.

And I made a rural pen,
And I stain'd the water clear,
And I wrote my happy songs
Every child may joy to hear

William Blake

SPRING

Sound the Flute!
Now it's mute.
Birds delight
Day and Night;
Nightingale
In the dale,
Lark in Sky,
Merrily,
Merrily, Merrily, to welcome in the Year.

Little Boy,
Full of joy;
Little Girl,
Sweet and small;
Cock does crow,
So do you;
Merry voice,
Infant noise,
Merrily, Merrily, to welcome in the Year.

Little Lamb,
Here I am;
Come and lick
My white neck;
Let me pull
Your soft Wool;
Let me kiss
Your soft face:
Merrily, Merrily, we welcome in the Year.

William Blake

THE STREET MUSICIAN

(based on the words of a song by Schubert)

With plaintive fluting, sad and slow,
   The old man by the roadside stands.
Who would have thought such notes could flow
   From such cracked lips and withered hands?

On shivering legs he stoops and sways,
   And not a passer stops to hark;
No penny cheers him as he plays;
   About his feet the mongrels bark.

But piping through the bitter weather,
   He lets the world go on its way.
Old piper! let us go together,
   And I will sing and you shall play.

James Reeves

VI. Brass and Percussion

Into Mother's slide trombone
Liz let fall her ice cream cone.
Now when marching, Mother drips
Melting notes and chocolate chips.

X. J. Kennedy

An old trumpeter out in L.A.
Played his horn seven hours a day
He triple tongued myriads
Of parallel triads
Till he drove all his neighbors away.

Carole Schoneman

LEWIS HAS A TRUMPET

A trumpet
A trumpet
Lewis has a trumpet
A bright one that's yellow
A loud proud horn.
He blows it in the evening
When the moon is newly rising
He blows it when it's raining
In the cold and misty morn
It honks and it whistles
It roars like a lion
It rumbles like a lion
With a wheezy huffing hum
His parents say it's awful
Oh really simply awful
But
Lewis says he loves it
It's such a handsome trumpet
And when he's through with trumpets
He's going to buy a drum.

Karla Kuskin

Said a hornist from lower Jerome,
"I'll never again play in Nome.
My embrouchure froze
In a tight-cornered pose
And no smiling until I got home."

Carole Schoneman

There was an Old Man with a gong,
Who bumped at it all the day long;
    But they called out, "O law!
    You're a horrid old bore!"
So they smashed that Old Man with a gong.

Edward Lear

RAIN

Like a drummer's brush,
the rain hushes the surfaces of tin porches.

Emanuel di Pasquale

CHOIR TRYOUTS

I hear birds. I sing frogs.
My heart hears every note,
Yet my song is locked
Inside my throat.
Someone laughs,
I'm way off-key.

The teacher holds my hand
And opens a special box
Of things with secret voices.

I get maracas and triangle.
I am aria. I am madrigal.
With silver bells and tambourine
        I can sing!

Kristine O'Connell George

TAMBOURINES

Tambourines!
Tambourines!
Tambourines
To the glory of God!
Tambourines
To glory!

A gospel shout
And a gospel song:
Life is short
But God is long!

Tambourines!
Tambourines!
Tambourines
To glory!

Langston Hughes

A bugler named Dougal MacDougal
Found ingenious ways to be frugal.
    He learned how to sneeze
    In various keys,
Thus saving the price of a bugle.

Ogden Nash

TAPS AT ARLINGTON, DAY GROVE AND PLEASANT HILL

They despise the young trumpeter,
blonde and breathing,
in the midst of their memories—
his half-familiar face
and unfaded uniform.

Every visit he repeats
a practiced elegy:
all is well, day is done—

Each note rings
like a clean shot.

Cynthia Pederson

HOW HIGH THE MOON

(first the melody, clean and hard,
and the flat slurs are faint;
the downknotted mouth, tugged in deprecation,
is not there. But near the end of the first chorus
the slurs have come
with the street of the quiet pogrom:
the beat of the street talk flares strong,
the scornful laughter and the gestures cut the air.)

"Blow! Blow!" the side-men cry,

and the thin black young man with an old man's face
lungs up
the tissue of a trumpet from his deep-cancered corners,
racks out a high and searing curse!
     Full from the sullen grace of his street it sprouts:
          NEVER YOUR CAPTIVE!

Lance Jeffers

From THE PRINCESS

The splendour falls on castle walls
    And snowy summits old in story:
The long light shakes across the lakes,
    And the wild cataract leaps in glory,
Blow, bugle, blow, set the wild echoes flying,
Blow, bugle; answer, echoes, dying, dying, dying.

    O hark, O hear! how thin and clear,
    And thinner, clearer, farther going!
O sweet and far from cliff and scar
    The horns of Elfland faintly blowing!
Blow, let us hear the purple glens replying:
Blow, bugle; answer, echoes, dying, dying, dying.

    O love, they die in yon rich sky,
    They faint on hill or field or river:
Our echoes roll from soul to soul,
    And grow for ever and for ever.
Blow, bugle, blow, set the wild echoes flying,
And answer, echoes, answer, dying, dying, dying.

Alfred, Lord Tennyson

VII. Time to Practice

INVOLUNTARY MUSIC

I practiced the piano all afternoon
while the others played ball.
As I memorized the notes
stepping out of my mind
in time, each harmony
abolishing the one before,
I could hear the crack of wood,
the bench applauding,
the batter squealing with delight:
then I resumed climbing
the ladder of the minor scale
broken at the third and seventh rung.
I tucked my thumb under my middle finger
and rose to the top, and once, my hand
travelled off the keys and paced
mechanically over the black walnut casing
and dropped, and I'd come to silence:
very far away, I heard
the triplewound metronome
and the scuff of bases being dragged home.

D. Nurkse

MUSIC MOTHER

I am twelve years old, my hair in braids,
my pedal feet in Oxfords.
I practice my scales, stepping up ivory.
Only the music, the metronome's heart-beat,
and my teacher's voice are real, as I sit at the piano.
Playing Mozart, in Pittsburgh, Pennsylvania.

I love Mrs. Karenyi, my piano teacher.
My mother calls her a "blue-stocking," but she wears
ordinary nylons on her bony knees.
Great paintings cut from magazines
fill her staircase wall.
They are even in the bathroom.

Alone as I practice, I think of her, alone,
in her crisp, gray skirt and silky blouse.
She sits by a brass bed with a white cover, lilacs
in a vase by the table. She reads.

Sometimes she invites me to dinner,
chicken paprikash and dumplings her mother
made in Hungary, so perfect in silver bowls
at first I am afraid to eat.
Then she opens her phonograph, takes out a record,
tells me the great Landowska, just for me,
will now play Mozart on the clavichord.

Naomi Feigelson Chase

A MUSICAL FAMILY

I can play the piano
I am nearly three.
I can play the long white note
That Mum calls Middle C.

Dad can play the clarinet.
My sister plays the fiddle.
But I'm the one who hits the piano
Slap bang in the middle.

John Mole

PIANO PRACTICE

A doting father once there was
  Who loved his daughter Gerda,
Until she got the piano craze—
  Then how the passion stirred her!
Her fingers were wild elephants' feet,
  And as month after month he heard her
        He tried every way
        To stop her play
From bribery to murder.

One day when she was practising,
  He popped up behind and caught her
And dumped her in his wheelbarrow
  And carried her off to slaughter.
Tipping her into a well, he cried,
  "Hurrah! I've drowned my daughter!"
        But a voice from the well
        Rang out like a bell,
  "Aha—there isn't any water!"

Ian Serraillier

TIME TO PRACTICE

Well, here we go again.
The scale of G major with the right hand.
The scale of G major with the left hand.
The scale of G major with both hands together.
Then we can play "The Jolly Millstream"
(as though a piano can sound like a millstream,
if anyone has seen a millstream around this place)
when what we really want to do is to
fool around a little and
figure out how to make some music
sound like one of those concert artists on a
big stage, bounding up and down the keyboard,
and Leonard Bernstein conducting,
and lots of people in the audience applauding
and applauding and applauding.

Myra Cohn Livingston

SUMMER RECITAL

dusk
raps your knuckles
like an impatient piano teacher.

these memory songs
never learn
right tempo

so she kneads your shoulder
to the proper
two/four time
while the keys fly away from you
fumbling around
in the dark
for themselves

cicadas
outside the window
whistle for attention
signaling summer
almost up
as it ticks out
like a metronome
wound down

adagio, now adagio
as you try harder
to forget
what all these people
want you to know
want you to learn

again
now again
one and two
one and two
count it out
and again
count it out

until your time
runs down
until
your summer
runs
out

Cynthia Pederson

HIGHLAND, 1955

Six in the morning, a weekday in May,
Mother is asleep, dead tired—
five children in seven years.
Dad is in the kitchen rehearsing his music.

Back from Bataan, back to work
he sells insurance day and night.
Saturdays in spring he sings weddings
for extra money we always need.

His baritone voice
someday Dennis, my brother, will imitate so well
that company in another room will become quiet,
saying, "Sh, Bernie's singing."

But that is another story years away.
This is six in the morning, a weekday in May,
the kitchen windows wide open
and Mrs. Krause next door listening.

Later she will confide to Mother,
"I wish Art would sing to me in the morning
like Bernie does to you."

Kevin FitzPatrick

SO YOU WANT TO HEAR THE BLUES

Just give me a minute to get myself
warmed up, I've been working
on this act for years.

I've been humming *Stormy Weather*
since before I knew
what words meant;
imitating Billie in the shower.

All those shoo-op, shoo-ops
in the background,
all those acapella
ooh baby, babies . . .
that's been my voice.

I'm a sad C
played on second fret.
I'm the saxophone
that wails all night
outside your bedroom window.

Baby, this break
you've given me might
just be my big one. The way I play
it, heartache sounds so sweet.

For my greatest hits
I'll add your name
to my long list of credits,
just another man who helped me
discover everything I know.

Grace Bauer

TAKING VIOLIN AT SCHOOL

I open my case
tighten my bow
pluck a string to tune.
I love to listen to it chirp across the echoing room.

My friends are in class
reading about
a famous English king,
But I am training this wooden bird upon my arm to sing.

April Halprin Wayland

WHY I DIDN'T PRACTICE MY VIOLIN TODAY

When I opened the case
I heard a loud shout:
"Keep your hands to yourself.
Get lost. Get out."

Something bad might have happened
If I didn't obey,
So I slammed the case shut
And went out to play.

Daniel Slossberg

VIII. Other Instruments

REASONS FOR LOVING THE HARMONICA

Because it isn't harmonious;

Because it gleams like the chrome
      on a '57 Chevy's front grille;

Because it fits in a hobo's bandanna;

Because it tolerates spit;
a little spit means the music is fervent;

Because it's easily rigged
to a contraption that frees the human
      hands;

Because it's cynical, yet sings;

Because it sings breathing in.

Julie Kane

A boy who played tunes on a comb,
Had become such a nuisance at homb,
    That ma spanked him, and then—
    "Will you do it again?"
And he cheerfully answered her, "Nomb."

Anonymous

BOTTLE MUSIC

I

My lips are drawn, tight and thin.
I'm almost ready to begin.
Firmly—so I will not slip
I press against the glassy lip
Of one that's opened in an "O"
And breathing deeply, puff and blow.

II

My hands get wet from filling up
Eight bottles with a measuring cup.
Each one is fuller than the next.
I hold two spoons; my wrists are flexed
To move to make the music flow
By tapping gently down the row.

Anita Wintz

FIRST SONG

Then it was dusk in Illinois, the small boy
After an afternoon of carting dung
Hung on the rail fence, a sapped thing
Weary to crying. Dark was growing tall
And he began to hear the pond frogs all
Calling upon his ear with what seemed their joy.

Soon their sound was pleasant for a boy
Listening in the smoky dusk and the nightfall
Of Illinois, and then from the field two small
Boys came bearing cornstalk violins
And rubbed three cornstalk bows with resins,
And they set fiddling with them as with joy.

It was now fine music the frogs and the boys
Did in the towering Illinois twilight make
And into dark in spite of the right arm's ache
A boy's hunched body loved out of a stalk
The first song of his happiness, and the song woke
His heart to the darkness and into the sadness of joy.

Galway Kinnell

JUKE BOX LOVE SONG

I could take the Harlem night
And wrap around you,
Take the neon lights and make a crown,
Take the Lenox Avenue buses,
Taxis, subways,
And for your love song tone their rumble down.
Take Harlem's heartbeat,
Make a drumbeat,
Put it on a record, let it whirl,
And while we listen to it play,
Dance with you till day—
Dance with you, my sweet brown Harlem girl.

Langston Hughes

NO STATIC

dialing down the stations
tune in hot-shot rock
a compact sound companion
everywhere I walk

the beat gets in my blood
pounding down the street
plugged into my head
the music fuels my feet

walking with my radio
the city noises gone
the place between my ears
wall-to-wall song

Monica Kulling

UMBILICAL

You can take away my mother
you can take away my sister,
but don't take away
my little transistor.

I can do without sunshine,
I can do without Spring,
but I can't do without
my ear to that thing.

I can live without water,
in a hole in the ground,
but I can't live without
that sound that sound that sound that sOWnd.

Eve Merriam

Sneaking in on soundless sneakers
    While her weary folks relax,
Wanda tiptoes to the speakers,
    Twists the volume up to max.

Windows shatter. Did a rock
    Flung by hand destroy the glass?
No way. Just a blast of Bach—
    Smashing, that B Minor Mass.

X. J. Kennedy

THE TUNING FORK

Up this small stream I dropped
    a lodgepole twig:
it stuck at the lip of a falls,
    teetered and slid
and was swept back into an eddy.
    I nudged it free.

When it reaches you, lift it out,
    whang it against
the heel of your hand, and pull
    that flat A out
over the woodwinds and winds
    and dropping water.

John Ridland

There was an old person of Jodd,
Whose ways were perplexing and odd;
    She purchased a whistle,
    And sate on a thistle,
And squeaked to the people of Jodd.

Edward Lear

BALLOON-SELLER

Like colourful notes
In a major key,
My balloons make music
And air is free,
But the poor composer
Must ask his fee,
So buy a balloon
For 20p.

John Mole

A FAINT PULSE

"I find it symbolic
that we have eyelids
but no earlids."
Yehudi Menuhin

The corner accordion player
sang an elegy for her mother
in front of Marshall Fields
while the Chicago cold tugged
impatiently. I didn't listen
or dig out a dollar; I only
glanced at her straw smile.
"If my mother in heaven could see . . ."
revolved through the door and
past the perfume; piped music
primed to pry at my pocketbook
interrupted that toothless
snatch of song.

She was counting her coin-speckled case
when I circled back to the street.
In my memory: I have moved her
to a chair in front of a fire,
drawn in a couple half-grown boys
who rag at her as she darns an old sock
and hums; I have changed my step, turned
and dropped into an accordion case
the ten I didn't spend inside.

Cynthia Pederson

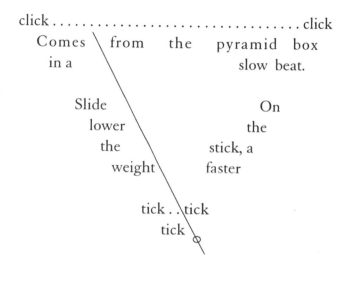

click . . . . click
    Comes \ from   the   pyramid box
      in a   slow beat.

     Slide   On
    lower   the
     the   stick, a
    weight \   faster

      tick . . \tick
       tick

    . . . . METRONOME

            Anita Wintz

IX. Other Musicians

BIRDSONG

If all birds
Have the same
Thing to say—

*This is my
Tree,* or *Please
Marry me*—

How is it
One's song rings
So silvery,

Another's scrapes
The air like
A rusty saw?

Valerie Worth

Repeat that, repeat,
Cuckoo, bird, and open ear wells, heart-springs,
    delightfully sweet,
With a ballad, with a ballad, a rebound
Off trundled timber and scoops of the hillside ground,
    hollow hollow hollow ground;
The whole landscape flushes on a sudden at a sound.

Gerard Manley Hopkins

MID-NOVEMBER CONCERT IN NEW JERSEY

After a long silence,
a few birds sing.
They're back, bluejay and
cardinal,
singing along with hardheaded leaves
that hang on high branches
and crick crack the wind,
singing as my sister and I,
half-drowned in red and
yellow fallen leaves,
join them with our shouts.

Emanuel di Pasquale

There were three little birds in a wood,
Who always sang hymns when they could.
What the words were about
They could never make out,
But they felt it was doing them good!

Anonymous

NEW MEXICO MUSIC

georgia o'keeffe
in new mexico
heard music
in the red hills
in the desert air
animal bones
sang
their clean notes
through her scorched
afternoons

in new mexico
georgia o'keeffe
let her brush
paint melodies
she
let her eye
see sound

Monica Kulling

SERENADE

The tin-type tune the locusts make,
Scarlatti-like, among the green
enameled grasses, plucking lutes
of parchment wing with plectrum leg,
ticks off in tones itinerant lives,
and tells in tryst-inviting trills
how love, in miniature modes
and minor forms, perpetuates
the constant, shapely themes of things,
and on melodic clocks records
a transient, true, and treasured bliss.

Dorothy Donnelly

GRASSHOPPER

silence

        stilled the meadow

  as if

      the cricket din

had stopped

     to hear

   the solo

        of

        the first

         violin

J. Patrick Lewis

RIVER

The river moans.
The river sings.

Listen to the Fox, the Menominee,
The Susquehanna, Colorado, Platte,
The Ottawa, Snake, Bear,
And the Delaware.

Listen to the river.
The river moans.
The river sings.

The river is always going home.

Lawrence Locke

SKIPPING STONES

Plink, plink, plink,
       plunk.
Plink, plink, plink, plink,
       plunk.
The small stones
              skim
the pond
dipping
       low
now and then
to play the water
like a green
          banjo
running lightly
          along
its strings
plucking out
an
       old
              wet
                     song.

Tony Johnston

FOREST HARPIST

Putting her hands to her harp—
There is a hush and the forest waits.
Fingers floating like shining fish scales down
Strings of foxtail and columbine.

Notes fall like rain, birdsong, waterfall.
Winds in the aspen trees
Leave forest floor shadows,
Rippling like piano keys.

Kristine O'Connell George

LULLABY

Softly, softly, softly croon,
Sing a whispered lullaby,
Learn the music from the moon
Moving still across the sky.

Sing a melody as tender
As the brook along the stones,
As the bees around the linden—
Humming, murmured, whispered tones.

Clemens Brentano
Translated by John W. Thomas

X. All Together

There was a young lady of Rio,
Who essayed to take part in a trio;
    But her skill was so scanty
    She played it andante
Instead of allegro con brio!

Anonymous

THE FIDDLERS

Nine feat fiddlers had good Queen Bess
To play her music as she did dress.
Behind an arras of horse and hound
They sate there scraping delightsome sound.
Spangled, bejewelled, her skirts would she
Draw o'er a petticoat of cramasie;
And soft each string like a bird would sing
In the starry dusk of evening.
Then slow from the deeps the crisscross bows,
Crooning like doves, arose and arose,
Till when, like a cage, her ladies did raise
A stiff rich splendour o'er her ribbed stays,
Like bumbling bees those four times nine
Fingers in melodies loud did pine;
Till came her coif and her violet shoon
And her virgin face shone out like the moon:
Oh, then in rapture those three times three
Fiddlers squealed shrill on their topmost C.

Walter de la Mare

117

From SONG FOR ST. CECILIA'S DAY

    Sharp violins proclaim
Their jealous pangs and desperation,
Fury, frantic indignation,
Depth of pains, and height of passion
    For the fair disdainful dame.

John Dryden

THE FLIGHT OF VAN BEETHOVEN

The conductor is dancing directions again.
These bees, these bees strive to please.

The stage is a hive, alive with buzzing violins
and attacking trombones. Their stingers thrust
into bassoons who only drone about going home,
going home. While horns—happy—hum and hum.

"This way," they all follow the wagging baton—
its circle dance left, its circle dance right.
That rise. Faster. Then down   down   hushing
into honey. It drips from flautists' lips
and is stored behind flying fingers:
Sweet Rachmaninoff. Luscious Ludwig.

Cynthia Pederson

IN THE CHURCH

In the church
the congregation is
singing songs of praise
raising their swaying arms
to Glory
Hallelujah they sing
going to give up their sins
give up their pain
going to start a new life
shed their old ways
at the altar
In the church
the congregation is swaying
singing songs of praise
raising their arms
and their voices
to Glory

Eloise Greenfield

CONCERT CHOIR

The first day we stood in gradations of high and low,
without sheet music; the director said we should just
listen to each other. In the pause after a piano chord,
there was expectancy, quiet without request.

He signalled the basses, and I was surprised that six boy-men
could roll a sound so low and full; then he added tenors,
a quiet shade above; then us, familiar warm resonance;
and finally those transparent high notes.

The slow-built chord hums in my chest, a ladder of notes
raised by breath and pulse, shimmering and complete.

Beth McGrath

CONCERT IN THE PARK

Streams of people hurry
over yellow-glazed bricks
criss-crossing Kliment Ohridski
Park just west of the university.
Moving along with them
under a bright October sky,
I start imagining
I'm hearing music then see
two little girls, brown hair flowing,
swaying to their three-quarter-size
violins, a case
invitingly open before them. Charmed
as I, many stoop to drop coins or bills;
more simply pause and listen. I rest
on a bench beneath sycamores, am enthralled.
Wild sweet music, loud and soft, floats
on a capricious wind
playing with clouds, sailing pigeons
and falling leaves.
                    Both hands high,
Kliment's statue reaches for fire
from his saintly teachers, Cyril and Methodius,
and stands aloof beyond
the musicians and their rapt audience.
Light suffusing linden leaves fills
my eyes; I bask in fall warmth,
music-awakened dreams, little
girls' songs.

Jim Thomas

THE MONEY CAME IN, CAME IN

My son Sam was a banjo man,
His brother played the spoons,
Willie Waley played the ukelele
And his sister sang the tunes:
      Sometimes sharp,
      Sometimes flat,
      It blew the top
      Off your Sunday hat,
      But no one bothered
      At a thing like that,
      And the money came in,
        came in.

Gussie Green played the tambourine,
His wife played the mandolin,
Tommy Liddell played a one-string
   fiddle
He made from a biscuit tin.
      Sometimes flat,
      Sometimes sharp,
      The noise was enough
      To break your heart,
      But nobody thought
      To cavil or carp,
      And the money came in,
        came in.

Clicketty Jones she played the bones,
Her husband the kettle-drum,
Timothy Tout blew the inside out
Of a brass euphonium.
Sometimes sharp,
Sometimes flat,
It sounded like somebody
Killing the cat,
But no one bothered
At a thing like that,
And the money came in,
came in.

Samuel Shute he played the flute,
His sister played the fife.
The Reverend Moon played a double
    bassoon
With the help of his lady wife.
Sometimes flat,
Sometimes sharp
As a pancake
Or an apple tart,
But everyone, everyone
Played a part
And the money came in,
came in.

Charles Causley

THE MUSIC MASTER

"My sons," said a Glurk slurping soup,
"We would make a fine musical group.
      Put your spoon to your lip
      And slurp when you sip,
But don't spill. Like this, children—Oop!"

John Ciardi

O MAGNIFICENT AND MANY

O magnificent and many:
The tambourines and drums we set up!
A thud and again a thud on them we make,
To delight our glorious ancestors.
It is for the descendant of T'ang that we play,
To assure that our ceremony is properly done.
The drumbeats reach far and deep;
Shrill, shrill is the music of the flutes:
Harmonious—ah yes—concordant
Together with our sonorous chimes of jade.
O grand great is T'ang's descendant;
Lovely and fine the symphony of his!
The bells and the drums are splendid;
The *wan* dance goes on gracefully.
We have a number of welcome guests:
None of them is less delighted than we.
Long since very old in the past,
With ancient people did all this rightly begin:
Be meek and mindful by day and night,
Everything we do let it be according to the rule.
May they turn to us and enjoy the offerings,
Which the descendant of T'ang has prepared!

Shih Ching
Translated by C. H. Wang

King T'ang, the founder of the Shang dynasty.
The *wan* dance was an elaborate ritual dance.

ENSEMBLE

Picasso painted
three musicians
in cubes of color
three instruments
clarinet
accordion
violin

sheet music ready

eyes that are
white holes
stare blankly
waiting
for their maestro
to say
"make music"

Monica Kulling

An extinct old ichthyosaurus
Once offered to sing in a chorus;
 But the rest of the choir
 Were obliged to retire,
His voice was so worn and sonorous.

Unknown

XI. Music in the Air

LISTENING TO A MONK FROM SHU PLAYING THE LUTE

A monk from Shu, carrying a precious lute,
Comes down from the western peak of Omei Mountain.
As he lifts his hands to play for me,
I seem to hear the sound of pines from a thousand glens.
The flowing stream cleanses a traveler's heart,
Its dying strains fade into the first bells of frost.
Dusk comes unnoticed over the green hills,
And autumn clouds begin to darken layer after layer.

Li Po
Translated by Joseph J. Lee

SEA/WINDS

How like the sounds of open seas—
the winds on all these trees.

Emanuel di Pasquale

From CHAMBER MUSIC, I

Strings in the earth and air
    Make music sweet;
Strings by the river where
    The willows meet.

There's music along the river
    For love wanders there,
Pale flowers on his mantle,
    Dark leaves on his hair.

All softly playing,
    With head to the music bent,
And fingers straying
    Upon an instrument.

James Joyce

THE GIVEN NOTE

On the most westerly Blasket
In a dry-stone hut
He got this air out of the night.

Strange noises were heard
By others who followed, bits of a tune
Coming in on loud weather

Though nothing like melody.
He blamed their fingers and ear
As unpractised, their fiddling easy

For he had gone alone into the island
And brought back the whole thing.
The house throbbed like his full violin.

So whether he calls it spirit music
Or not, I don't care. He took it
Out of wind off mid-Atlantic.

Still he maintains, from nowhere.
It comes off the bow gravely,
Rephrases itself into the air.

Seamus Heaney

DAYBREAK IN ALABAMA

When I get to be a composer
I'm gonna write me some music about
Daybreak in Alabama
And I'm gonna put the purtiest songs in it
Rising out of the ground like a swamp mist
And falling out of heaven like soft dew.
I'm gonna put some tall tall trees in it
And the scent of pine needles
And the smell of red clay after rain
And long red necks
And poppy colored faces
And big brown arms
And the field daisy eyes
Of black and white black white black people
And I'm gonna put white hands
And black hands and brown and yellow hands
And red clay earth hands in it
Touching everybody with kind fingers
And touching each other natural as dew
In that dawn of music when I
Get to be a composer
And write about daybreak
In Alabama.

Langston Hughes

Behind the beard
I hear Brahms smiling
as he stomps
out of his dark wood
hands behind his back
stomach forward
this man who made
the voice of sorrow
so understood.
Once in a while
I hear him smile.
What did he see
in the forest that morning—
a mouse riding a rabbit
a child playing dragon
or simply leaves laughing?

Julia Cunningham

THE DREAMING OF THE BONES

At the grey round of the hill
Music of a lost kingdom
Runs, runs and is suddenly still.
The winds out of Clare-Galway
Carry it: suddenly it is still.

I have heard in the night air
A wandering airy music;
And moidered in that snare
A man is lost of a sudden,
In that sweet wandering snare.

What finger first began
Music of a lost kingdom?
They dream that laughed in the sun.
Dry bones that dream are bitter.
They dream and darken our sun.

Those crazy fingers play
A wandering airy music;
Our luck is withered away
And wheat in the wheat-ear withered,
And the wind blows it away.

My heart ran wild when it heard
The curlew cry before dawn
And the eddying cat-headed bird;
But now the night is gone.
I have heard from far below
The strong March birds a-crow.
Stretch neck and clap the wing,
Red cocks, and crow!

William Butler Yeats

WINTER SONG

Singing.   Singing.
Where are the birds that are singing?

It has rained.   And still the branches
Have no new leaves.   Singing.   Birds
Are singing.   Where are the birds
That are singing?

I have no birds in cages.
There are no children who sell them.   Singing.
The valley is far away.   Nothing . . .

I do not know where the birds are
That are singing—singing, singing—
The birds that are singing.

Juan Ramón Jiménez
Translated by H. R. Hays

SOUTH AFRICAN BLOODSTONE
For Hugh Masekela

South African bloodstone
drenched with the soil
drenched with the beauty
of the drum-drum beat of land

drenched with the beauty
of God's first creation of man

& sculpted into lean hawk look
eyes burning deep
                    bold diamonds of fire
dance sing music to the air

Conjureman/conjure up
the rhythm of voodoo walk
weave the spell/paint the trance
begin the fire ritual

Hugh Masekela! homeboy
from the original home/going home
play your horn your trumpet horn
screech scream speak of ancestors

Conjureman/conjure up
the memory of ancestral lands
the easy walk the rhythmic walk
click click talk of trumpet genius

Hugh Masekela homeboy
from the original home going home

Speak South African bloodstone speak!

Quincy Troupe

MUSIC

Orpheus with his lute made trees,
   And the mountain-tops that freeze,
Bowed themselves when he did sing.
   To his music plants and flowers
Ever sprung: as sun and showers
   There had made a lasting spring.
Everything that heard him play,
   Even the billows of the sea,
Hung their heads, and then lay by.
   In sweet music is such art,
Killing care and grief of heart
   Fall asleep, or, hearing, die.

John Fletcher

From *THE TEMPEST*
Act 3, Scene 2

Be not afeard: the isle is full of noises,
Sounds and sweet airs, that give delight, and hurt not.
Sometimes a thousand twangling instruments
Will hum about mine ears; and sometimes voices,
That, if I then had wak'd after long sleep,
Will make me sleep again: and then, in dreaming,
The clouds methought would open and show riches
Ready to drop upon me; that, when I wak'd
I cried to dream again.

William Shakespeare

XII. All of Me Sings

WAY DOWN IN THE MUSIC

I get way down in the music
Down inside the music
I let it wake me
                take me
Spin me around and make me
Uh-get down

Inside the sound of the Jackson Five
Into the tune of Earth, Wind and Fire
Down in the bass where the beat comes from
Down in the horn and down in the drum
I get down
I get down

I get way down in the music
Down inside the music
I let it wake me
                take me
Spin me around and shake me
I get down, down
I get down

Eloise Greenfield

TO MUSIC. A SONG.

Music, thou *Queen of Heaven,* Care-charming-spell,
    That strikest a stillness into hell:
Thou that tamest *Tygers,* and fierce storms that rise
    With thy soul-melting Lullabies:
Fall down, down, down, from those thy chiming spheres,
To charm our souls, as thou enchantest our ears.

Robert Herrick

MUSIC BECOMES ME

as water
becomes the creek
trilling, filling it
giving it voice.

Music becomes me
like sparks
zipping
through electric wires
making light of dark.

Music becomes me
as wind
becomes the storm
swishing, swaying me
tapping my feet
thrusting my hands up
like castanets chattering.

Caught in its breath
I dance on winter's roof.

Marni McGee

MAKE MUSIC WITH YOUR LIFE

Make music with your life
a
      jagged
silver tune
cuts every deepday madness
Into jewels   that you wear

Carry 16 bars of old blues
wit/you
everywhere you go
walk thru azure sadness
howlin
Like a guitar player

Bob O'Meally

HEART MUSIC

```
   umpsingfl            psingfl
  oundthumpsing.        oundthumpsing
  lutterpoundthump.    flutterpoundthum
 thumpsingflutterpoundthumpsingflutterp
rpoundthumpsingflutterpoundthumpsingflut
gflut        thumpsingflutt.       humps
dthumpsingflutterpoundthump ingflutterpc
rpoundthumpsingflutterpound  umpsingflut
gflutterpoundthumpsingflutt   oundthumps
thumpsingflutterpoundthumps    gflutterp
 oundthumpsingflut  rpoundthumpsingfl
  utterpoundthump   flutterpoundthu
   mpsingflutterp   thumpsingflut
    thumpsinglu  o  poundthumps
     poundthumps. gflutterpo
      flutterpoundthumpsir
        ingflutterpound
         umpsingflu
          ound
```

Anita Wintz

ON RACHMANINOFF'S BIRTHDAY

Blue windows, blue rooftops
and the blue light of the rain,
there contiguous phrases of Rachmaninoff
pouring into my enormous ears
and the tears falling into my blindness

for without him I do not play,
especially in the afternoon
on the day of his birthday. Good
fortune, you would have been
my teacher and I your only pupil

and I would always play again.
Secrets of Liszt and Scriabin
whispered to me over the keyboard
on unsunny afternoons! and growing
still in my stormy heart.

Only my eyes would be blue as I played
and you rapped my knuckles,
          dearest father of all the Russias,
          placing my fingers
tenderly upon your cold, tired eyes.

Frank O'Hara

THE WEARY BLUES

Droning a drowsy syncopated tune,
Rocking back and forth to a mellow croon,
    I heard a Negro play.
Down on Lenox Avenue the other night
By the pale dull pallor of an old gas light
    He did a lazy sway . . .
    He did a lazy sway . . .
To the tune o' those Weary Blues.
With his ebony hands on each ivory key
He made that poor piano moan with melody.
    O Blues!
Swaying to and fro on his rickety stool
He played that sad raggy tune like a musical fool.
    Sweet Blues!
Coming from a black man's soul.
    O Blues!
In a deep song voice with a melancholy tone
I heard that Negro sing, that old piano moan—
    "Ain't got nobody in all this world,
    Ain't got nobody but ma self.
    I's gwine to quit ma frownin'
    And put ma troubles on de shelf."
Thump, thump, thump, went his foot on the floor.

He played a few chords then he sang some more—
    "I got de Weary Blues
    And I can't be satisfied.
    Got de Weary Blues
    And can't be satisfied
    I ain't happy no mo'
    And I wish that I had died."
And far into the night he crooned that tune.
The stars went out and so did the moon.
The singer stopped playing and went to bed.
While the Weary Blues echoed through his head
He slept like a rock or a man that's dead.

Langston Hughes

THE CONDUCTOR'S HANDS

See the magic music glisten
    in his quick magician's hands;
music flickers in his fingers,
    watch him weave it into strands
of sound he wraps around you
    from your ankles to your hair;
mesmerized by silver sound, you
    watch him pluck the notes from air.

Alice Schertle

RECORD

I think I know just how the notes should sound,
And yet there's always something in the way
The violins, the horns and woodwinds play
That makes me understand that I have found

A kind of hearing that is strange and new,
A music I have never heard before,
And so I listen, listen more,
Asking what it is that Mozart knew

That I must find myself, and hear, although
The next time that I play it, some new phrase
Will whirl within my head for days and days
And come to be a part of all I know.

Myra Cohn Livingston

TO MUSIC, TO BECALM HIS FEVER

Charm me asleep, and melt me so
    With thy Delicious Numbers;
That being ravished, hence I go
    Away in easy-slumbers.
       Ease my sick head,
       And make my bed,
Thou Power that canst sever
       From me this ill:
       And quickly still:
       Though thou not kill
       My Fever.

Robert Herrick

BEETHOVEN'S DEATH MASK

I imagine him still with heavy brow.
Huge, black, with bent head and falling hair,
He ploughs the landscape. His face
Is this hanging mask transfigured,
This mask of death which the white lights make stare.

I see the thick hands clasped; the scare-crow coat;
The light strike upwards at the holes for eyes;
The beast squat in that mouth, whose opening is
The hollow opening of an organ pipe:
There the wind sings and the harsh longing cries.

He moves across my vision like a ship.
What else is iron but he? The fields divide
And, heaving, are changing waters of the sea.
He is prisoned, masked, shut off from Being.
Life, like a fountain, he sees leap—outside.

Yet, in that head there twists the roaring cloud
And coils, as in a shell, the roaring wave.
The damp leaves whisper; bending to the rain
The April rises in him, chokes his lungs
And climbs the torturing passage of his brain.

Then the drums move away, the Distance shows:
Now cloud-hid peaks are bared; the mystic One
Horizons haze, as the blue incense, heaven.
Peace, peace . . . Then splitting skull and dream, there comes
Blotting our lights, the Trumpeter, the sun.

Stephen Spender

Index of Authors

Index of Titles

Index of First Lines

Index of Translators

ACKNOWLEDGMENTS

THE EDITOR AND PUBLISHER THANK THE FOLLOWING FOR PERMISSION TO REPRINT THE COPYRIGHTED MATERIAL LISTED BELOW. EVERY EFFORT HAS BEEN MADE TO LOCATE ALL PERSONS HAVING ANY RIGHTS OR INTERESTS IN THE MATERIAL PUBLISHED HERE. ANY EXISTING RIGHTS NOT HERE ACKNOWLEDGED WILL, IF THE EDITOR OR PUBLISHER IS NOTIFIED, BE DULY ACKNOWLEDGED IN FUTURE EDITIONS OF THIS BOOK.

LLOYD ALEXANDER for his translations of "Autumn Song" by Paul Verlaine and "The Flute" by André Chénier, copyright © 1995 by Lloyd Alexander.

GEORGE W. BAHLKE for "Birdsong" by Valerie Worth. Copyright © 1995 by George W. Bahlke.

GRACE BAUER for "So You Want to Hear the Blues," copyright © 1989 by Grace Bauer.

WILLIS CARMER BAILEY, DORIS BAILEY GIBBS, and MRS. KINGSLEY MOORE for "Slave Quarter" by Carl Carmer from French Town.

BEACON PRESS for "Ray Charles" from Generations by Sam Cornish, copyright © 1968, 1969, 1970, 1971 by Sam Cornish. Reprinted by permission of Beacon Press.

A. R. BEAL, literary executor for James Reeves, for "My Singing Aunt," "The Piano," and "The Street Musician" from Complete Poems for Children by James Reeves. London: Heinemann. Copyright © 1973 by James Reeves.

NAOMI FEIGELSON CHASE for "Music Mother," copyright © 1980 by Naomi Feigelson Chase.

MADELEINE COMORA for "Cello," copyright © 1995 by Madeleine Comora.

JULIA CUNNINGHAM for "Behind the beard," "Lullaby," and "Museum Violin," copyright © 1995 by Julia Cunningham.

EMANUEL DI PASQUALE for "Mid-November Concert in New Jersey," "Rain," and "Sea/Winds," copyright © 1995 by Emanuel di Pasquale.

JOSEPH F. DOMINGUEZ for his translations of "Cada vez que tengo penas," "El tambor es tu retrato," "Esta guitarra que toco," and "Si me pongo yo a cantar," copyright © 1995 by Joseph F. Domínguez.

FABER AND FABER LIMITED for "The Given Note" from Door into the Dark by Seamus Heaney. Copyright © 1995 by Seamus Heaney. "Beethoven's Death Mask" from Collected Poems 1928–1985 by Stephen Spender. Copyright © 1995 by Stephen Spender.

FARRAR, STRAUS & GIROUX, INC. for "Mama's Song" from Balloons and Other Poems by Deborah Chandra. Copyright © 1988, 1990 by Deborah Chandra. "My Voice" and "Winter Song" from Selected Writing of Juan Ramón Jiménez translated by H. R. Hays. Copyright ©1957 by Juan Ramón Jiménez and copyright renewed © 1985 by Farrar, Straus & Giroux, Inc. "Banjo Tune" from Laughing Time: Collected Nonsense by William Jay Smith. Copyright ©1990 by William Jay Smith. Reprinted by permission of Farrar, Straus & Giroux, Inc.

KEVIN FITZPATRICK for "Highland 1955," copyright © 1987 by Kevin FitzPatrick.

THE ANGEL FLORES ESTATE for "The Guitar" by Federico García Lorca and "Tavern Guitar Playing a Jota Today" by Joaquim Maria Machado from An Anthology of Spanish Poetry, edited by Angel Flores. Copyright © 1961.

KRISTINE O'CONNELL GEORGE for "Choir Tryouts," "Dog and Papa's Fiddle," and "Forest Harpist," copyright © 1995 by Kristine O'Connell George.

GROVE/ATLANTIC, INC. for "On Rachmaninoff's Birthday" from Meditations in an Emergency by Frank O'Hara. Copyright © 1957 by Frank O'Hara. Used by permission of Grove/Atlantic, Inc.

DONALD HALL for his translation of "The Six Strings" by Federico García Lorca. Copyright © 1982 by Donald Hall.

HARPERCOLLINS PUBLISHERS for "Way Down in the Music" from Honey, I Love by Eloise Greenfield. Copyright © 1978 by Eloise Greenfield. "Gertrude" from Bronzeville Boys and Girls by Gwendolyn Brooks. Copyright © 1956 by Gwendolyn Brooks Blakely. "Lewis Has a Trumpet" from Dogs & Dragons, Trees & Dreams by Karla Kuskin. Copyright © 1958 by Karla Kuskin. Selections reprinted by permission of HarperCollins Publishers.